Small Fur

by IRINA KORSCHUNOW

with pictures by REINHARD MICHL

translated from the German
by JAMES SKOFIELD

HARPER & ROW, PUBLISHERS

Small Fur

Library of Congress Cataloging-in-Publication Data
Korschunow, Irina.
Small fur.

Translation of: Kleiner Pelz.
Summary: After losing his best friend, Small Fur
meets an elf and has an incredible adventure before
he finds a new best friend.
    [1. Elves—Fiction.   2. Friendship—Fiction]
I. Michl, Reinhard, ill.   II. Title.
PZ7.K8376Sm   1988   [E]   87-45289
ISBN 0-06-023247-1
ISBN 0-06-023248-X (lib. bdg.)

Small Fur

It was a beautiful, sunny day. Raspberries were ripening in the forest. Young birds were flying out of their nests in search of food. It was a happy day. Only Small Fur was sad.

Small Fur wasn't really his name. His real name was Coal Fur. But he was so soft and snuggly when he was born that his mother called him Small Fur. And the name stuck. Now everyone called him Small Fur. The neighbors. Aunt Grouch. And Brown Fur.

6

Brown Fur lived nearby. He was a little bigger and a little stronger than Small Fur, and he was his best friend. Small Fur had learned a lot from him—how to leap over streams; how to hide from fog witches, cave trolls and tree ghosts; how to catch fish and find honey; how to tell the difference between good berries and poison berries; and much, much more.

They played ball together. They built treehouses and chased squirrels. They counted the stars in the night sky together. Sometimes they agreed, sometimes they disagreed and quarreled. But they always made up, as all good friends do.

But now Brown Fur was moving to another forest. The moving van was in front of his house. Small Fur stood watching the moving van get fuller and fuller and the house get emptier and emptier.

"Why don't you stay?" he asked Brown Fur.

"How can I?" asked Brown Fur, and he was sad too.

When the last chair had been loaded, Brown Fur climbed into the back of the moving van and the van pulled away. Brown Fur sat there, holding his big red ball.

"Brown Fur!" called Small Fur.

"Good-bye!" called Brown Fur. He threw him his ball. "It's yours!"

And the moving van disappeared into the trees and bushes.

"Brown Fur!" called Small Fur again.

But only the blackbirds rustled
8 in the branches.

Sadly Small Fur picked up the red ball and walked home through the forest alone. His cap was left hanging on a tree branch. He trudged through the puddles. Blackberry thorns tore his pants. Small Fur didn't notice a thing.

9

Aunt Grouch was standing at the front door.
Aunt Grouch came for a visit each summer,
10   and she always stayed much longer.

"Late again, Small Fur," she grumbled. "Just look at your pants! And where's your new cap? You lose everything. Disgraceful!"

Small Fur ran to his mother.

"Make Aunt Grouch go away," he said.

"She means no harm!" said Mother. "But you really are very late. And you should take better care of your things. You can't go on losing something every day."

"Brown Fur has gone away," said Small Fur.

His mother took him into her arms and hugged him tight.

Later, when Small Fur was in bed, she told him stories about elves.

His mother told him stories almost every night. She told him stories about fog witches, water goblins, tree ghosts and trolls, and sometimes she told him about the big Nock who lives deep down in the black pool. Sometimes Small Fur was a little scared and held on to his mother's hand tightly. But the stories about elves weren't scary. Elves had wings and you could see through them. Small Fur wasn't afraid of elves.

"What do elves do all day?" asked Small Fur.

"You know what they do," said his mother. "They fly. They fly over forests and meadows and rivers."

"I want to fly too," said Small Fur.

"We are not transparent and we do not have wings," said Mother. "We cannot fly."

"But I want to fly so much," said Small Fur. "I want to see the trees, and the river, and our house. And I could look for Brown Fur."   13

"Go to sleep, Small Fur," said Mother.

"Where do elves live?" asked Small Fur. "In our forest?"

"Everywhere," said Mother. "You know elves don't let themselves be seen. Good night, Small Fur. Sleep well."

She hugged him, turned off the light and left.

Small Fur lay in bed with his eyes wide open. He thought about the moving van that had disappeared into the trees. He thought about playing alone in the forest. He thought about Brown Fur and Aunt Grouch and the elves with their wings.

When he finally fell asleep, he dreamed about flying.

He dreamed he flew over forests and meadows and rivers. The wind carried him higher and higher into the sky, and it was wonderful.

15

In the morning, Small Fur had forgotten his dream. He got up and pulled on his pants. The sun was shining, but Small Fur was not happy.

Mother and Aunt Grouch were having break-fast in the kitchen.

"Morning," said Small Fur.

"*Good* morning, you mean," said Aunt Grouch. "Did you wash your ears?"

"No," said Small Fur.

"Well, wash them," said Aunt Grouch. "Ears must be washed every day if one is to hear properly."

"I haven't washed my ears for three days, and I can hear perfectly," said Small Fur.

Aunt Grouch sputtered until Small Fur's mother took a wet washcloth and washed his ears. By the time she was done, Small Fur was not hungry.

"Now eat your honeybread," said Aunt Grouch, "or you will not grow up to be as big as I am."

Small Fur threw his honeybread facedown on the table.

"I don't want to grow up," he said. "I don't want to be like you."

Aunt Grouch sputtered and fumed and puffed up like a balloon.

"You really are being very naughty," said Mother. "I don't want to hug you anymore."

18   "I don't care," said Small Fur.

He took his red ball and went into the woods. He was much sadder than the day before.

When he got to Brown Fur's house, he screwed his eyes shut. I'll count to five, he thought. Maybe then Brown Fur will come back.

But Brown Fur didn't come back.

Small Fur sat down on the moss. He held his ball tight and stared at the spot between the trees and bushes where the moving van had disappeared.

Suddenly he saw a gate between the trees, a big green gate. It led to a meadow filled with flowers—blue and red and yellow. At the end of the meadow, there were birch trees.

Small Fur could not believe his eyes. He knew every clearing, every tree, and he had never seen this meadow or these birch trees. Quickly, he got up, and walked through the gate.

The air smelled sweet. Small Fur sniffed the flowers. They smelled like honey. Small Fur licked the blossoms with the tip of his tongue. They tasted like honey. Honeyflowers.

Small Fur wanted to pick a honeyflower for his mother, but then he remembered his mother didn't want to hug him anymore. And he certainly didn't want Aunt Grouch to enjoy the honeyflowers.

20

21

Small Fur walked past the flowers and across the meadow toward the birch trees. He came to a pool of black water. He didn't want to stay there, so he walked on.

It was light and quiet among the trees. Only the leaves rustled in the breeze.

Then he saw the elf! She was sitting on a gray rock. She was crying, her face hidden in her hands.

Small Fur knew she was an elf the minute he saw her. She had wings! Anyone who had wings had to be an elf.

Small Fur waited awhile.

Then he went over to the rock and whispered, "Hello, elf."

The elf raised her head and looked at him. She was just as small and snuggly as he was. But she was transparent. Transparent as glass.

"Who are you?" she asked.

Small Fur didn't answer right away.

"Small Fur," he finally said. "Well, *Coal* Fur, really, but I like Small Fur better."

"Where do you come from?"

"From over there." Small Fur pointed with his thumb to the honeyflower meadow. "Through the gate."

"Through the gate? You found the green gate?" The elf slid down from the rock, and Small Fur noticed she was missing a wing.

"Where's your other wing?" he asked.

23

"The Nock stole it," said the elf. "The horrible Nock did it when he tried to pull me into his dark pool. And now I can't fly. Ever again."

She started to cry again. Small Fur wanted to hug her, but he didn't know if you could hug an elf.

He sat down near the rock and waited. The sun rose higher and the ground grew warm. The woods smelled of mushrooms and rasp-

berries. Small Fur thought about lunch, and was about to go home when the elf said, "I know why you found the green gate. You are here to help me."

"Me?" asked Small Fur, surprised.

"Yes, you," said the elf. "You must go to the Nock and bring back my wing."

Small Fur jumped up. "Not me, no! I sometimes used to help Brown Fur when he got stuck in a rabbit hole or lost his ball. But I can't help an elf. You have to find someone bigger and stronger."

The elf took his hand.

"Please help me, Small Fur, or I'll never be able to fly again, and flying is the most wonderful thing in the world."

Small Fur could hear his heart pounding.

"I want to fly very much, too," he said.

"Then go to the Nock and bring back my wing," said the elf. "When I have both my wings, I will lend them to you. Then you can fly with the wind, as far as you wish." 25

Small Fur thought about his dream, and his heart pounded even louder. To fly! Over forests and meadows and rivers. And to look for Brown Fur!

"Go to the Nock," repeated the elf.

"But I don't know him," said Small Fur. "And the Nock doesn't know me, either."

"There is a call," said the elf. "If the Nock hears it, he'll come up to the surface.

"Nock, Nock, Nock, deep-water king,
Nock, Nock, Nock, you wet old thing,
Leave your cold pool, black as night,
Show your green face to the light."

Small Fur scratched himself.

"Did you ever use the Nock call?" he asked.

"No," said the elf. "We elves are afraid of the Nock. That is why you have to do it."

Small Fur scratched himself again. He itched all over. "Nerve fleas" his mother called it.

"First I must go home for lunch," he said. "Or my Aunt Grouch will really grumble. And after that we have to pick raspberries. But maybe I'll come back tomorrow."

"Do you promise?" asked the elf.

Small Fur looked down.

"Don't tell anyone you came here," said the elf. "If you do, you will never find the green gate again. Then the Nock will keep my wing, and you will never fly."

The minute Small Fur walked into the house, he could smell herb soup. He loved herb soup and began to eat it right away.

"Not so fast," grumbled Aunt Grouch, "or you'll spill something again."

Suddenly Small Fur's elbow bumped his cup. Red juice spilled all over the tablecloth.

"What did I tell you !" shrieked Aunt Grouch.

Mother sighed. "Can't we ever eat in peace?" she asked.

After that, the soup tasted only half as good.

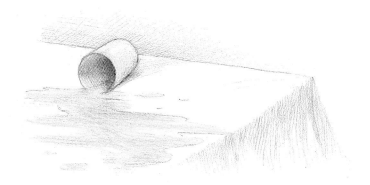

When they went raspberry picking, Aunt Grouch kept right on grumbling: Small Fur was too slow; he popped too many berries into his mouth; he left the plumpest berries on the bushes. Small Fur was so upset, he tripped over a root and his bucket went tumbling. Raspberries went rolling every which way.

"It's all right," said Mother. She laughed. "The worms will be very happy."

Small Fur didn't laugh. He stomped on the raspberries and shouted, "It's all Aunt Grouch's fault!"

And Aunt Grouch said, "I've never seen such a rude and clumsy furchild."

Tomorrow, I'll go see the elf, thought Small Fur. I will call the Nock and get back the elf's wing, and then I'll fly to Brown Fur and never come back. 29

That night Small Fur didn't want to hear any stories. He closed his eyes tightly and pretended he was asleep. His mother hugged him. But he wouldn't open his eyes.

The next morning, Small Fur had to watch the raspberry jam to make sure it didn't boil over. He stood on the stool, holding the cooking spoon firmly in his hand, and stirred the jam. He stirred until his arm hurt.

Mother came and hugged him.

"It's done," she said. "Now you can go and play."

"Work never hurt anybody," said Aunt Grouch.

"Nasty Aunt Grouch," said Small Fur, loudly.

The hugs stopped once again.

31

Small Fur took his ball and ran to the green gate. The honeyflowers smelled sweet. And there was the elf, waiting for him.

"We have to hurry," she said. "The sun is still shining on the black pool. When the shadows fall on it, the Nock will go to sleep and will not hear you."

She took his hand and led him past the birch trees to the pool with the dark water.

"This is the black pool," she whispered. "*He* lives here. The Nock."

Smooth and still the pool lay in the sunlight. A dragonfly zipped over the water.

"Do you remember the call?" whispered the elf.

Small Fur nodded.

"What will I tell the Nock?" he asked.

"I don't know. You'll think of something," said the elf. "Just remember, if you bring back my wing I will let you fly, over forests and meadows and rivers, wherever you want to."

She spun around.

"Don't go!" cried Small Fur.

But the elf was gone.

Small Fur stood alone by the Nock's pool. The water glinted like a dark stone. There was not even a ripple on it. No bush or tree let its branches dip down to it.

"Nock," whispered Small Fur.

Nothing moved.

"Nock," Small Fur called, a little louder....

"Nock, Nock, Nock, deep-water king,
Nock, Nock, Nock, you wet old thing,
Leave your cold pool, black as night,
Show your green face to the light."

Bubbles rose from deep below and burst on the surface. The water gurgled and bubbled, and then a head broke the surface, a green head covered with waterweeds.

"You called me?" gurgled the Nock.

Small Fur drew back.

"Who are you?" asked the Nock, and swam closer to the edge.

Small Fur was about to tell him his name, but he stopped because the Nock began to climb out of the water—huge and green and weedy.

"No!" screamed Small Fur. He tried to run, but the Nock stretched out his arm and held him fast. Small Fur fell on the grass. He lay there, hardly breathing.

The Nock bent over him.

"Don't run away," he said. "Stay with me. I am so alone in my black pool."

He stroked Small Fur's nose and chin with his green finger.

"You called me. What do you want?"

Small Fur looked up at the weedy face.

The Nock didn't look mean. He smiled, and Small Fur wasn't frightened anymore. He stood up and said, "My name is Small Fur. The elf sent me. I came to get the wing you stole from her."

"Stole?" cried the Nock. "I didn't mean to steal her wing. I only wanted to talk with her for a while. Why did she run away?"

"The elves are afraid of you," said Small Fur.

39

The Nock shook his head, and water drops spattered Small Fur's face.

"I don't mean the elves any harm. I only want to sit with them on the bank and talk and not be so lonely. Why doesn't anyone believe me?"

He gurgled and burbled to himself. It sounded as if he was going to cry. Small Fur would gladly have hugged him, but he didn't dare.

"I am lonely, too," he said. "That's why I need the wing. When I bring the elf her wing, she'll let me fly. Please, Nock, give me her wing."

"Fly?" The Nock shook his head again. "Why do you want to fly? I can't fly either. I belong in the water, the elves belong in the air and *you* belong in the forest."

Small Fur thought about that.

"I must find Brown Fur," he said.

They sat down by the pond and talked.

The Nock told him about his silver fish and his water-lily garden. Small Fur told him about Brown Fur. He also told him about Aunt Grouch and all her grumbling, and that his mother had stopped hugging him.

The Nock listened. The weedy hair tumbled over his green face.

"Poor Small Fur," he said. "You are all alone and I am all alone. Will you come and live with me in my black pool?"

Small Fur was so surprised, he dropped his ball. He almost fell into the water.

"No, Nock, no! The water is too wet. I don't like water. Everyone knows that."

The Nock looked at him sadly. "You're afraid of me, too," he said.

"I cannot breathe underwater," cried Small Fur. "I belong in the forest—you said so yourself."

"Nothing bad will happen to you in my black pool if *I* invite you," said the Nock. "Visit me for a while. Just for this afternoon. Maybe then the elves will stop being afraid of me." He slid back into the water.

"Come," he called. "Come with me and I'll give you back the wing."

What do I do now? thought Small Fur. I don't want to go. But all the same, he closed his eyes, clutched his red ball close to him and jumped in after the Nock.

At first it was dark, wet and *very* cold. But gradually it got lighter and warmer. Small Fur found himself in front of a house made of seaweed, moss, and shining stones. The Nock was waiting for him by the door.

"Welcome to my black pool, Small Fur," said the Nock, and he led him through the silent green rooms. He showed him the silver fish and the water-lily garden, and they played ball in the hills and valleys at the bottom of the pool. When Small Fur got hungry, the Nock gave him green cake. It tasted strange. Quite different from his mother's cake, and not half as good.

Time passed. Shadows fell on the black pool.

"It's time for me to go to sleep, Small Fur." The Nock yawned. "You can leave whenever you want to. Or would you rather stay with me?" The Nock patted Small Fur's face with his weedy hand.

"I want to go home," said Small Fur. "Don't be sad, Nock. I'll come back soon."

Suddenly it got dark, wet and *very* cold. Then just as suddenly it got light and dry and warm.

Small Fur found himself sitting by the side of the pool holding his ball as if nothing had happened. But in his hand was the wing—transparent as glass and shimmering like a rainbow, blue, red, green and yellow.

Slowly, Small Fur got up.

Now I can fly! he thought, and he rushed over to the gray rock, where the elf was waiting for him.

"Thank you, Small Fur," she said.

"When can I fly?" he asked.

"You can fly when the sun is shining," said the elf.

Small Fur sat down beside her and told her about the water-lily garden, about the hills and valleys deep in the black pool, and that he had played ball with the Nock.

"The Nock isn't mean," he said. "He is just sad and lonely. You must visit him, that would make him happy." The elf nodded, and Small Fur stayed with her until it got dark.

"You can fly tomorrow," said the elf. "But

don't tell anyone about our gate, or you'll
never find it again."

Small Fur's mother was in the kitchen. She had made Small Fur's favorite raspberry pancakes. Small Fur sprinkled sugar and cinnamon on them and licked his lips.

"I'm glad you're back," said his mother.

Small Fur was also glad. That is, until Aunt Grouch came in and said, "Stop munching so loudly." Small Fur cleaned his plate quickly and went to bed.

Tomorrow I will fly, he thought. Maybe I'll dream about it tonight. But instead Small Fur dreamed about raspberry pancakes.

It rained during the night, and it was still raining the next morning.

"It will last three days," grumbled Aunt Grouch.

"Oh, it will soon stop," said Mother.

After lunch, the sun finally came out. Small Fur took his ball and ran outside.

He looked hopefully over at Brown Fur's house
as he always did. Someone *was* standing in

front of it, holding a ball!

"Brown Fur!" yelled Small Fur, and started running. But it wasn't Brown Fur. It was another furchild. And the ball was yellow.

"Hi," said the furchild, and smiled.

"Hi," said Small Fur. "Who are you?"

"Curly Fur. What's your name?"

"Small Fur," said Small Fur. "Well, *Coal* Fur, really, but nobody calls me that. Do you live here now?"

"Yes," said Curly Fur, "since this morning."

"Brown Fur used to live here," said Small Fur. "He gave me this ball."

"Do you like to play ball?" asked Curly Fur. Small Fur nodded.

"Me, too," said Curly Fur.

"Let's play!"

They ran about and played ball together.

"There are fish in the brook," said Small Fur. "Do you want me to show you how to catch them? But you have to be careful. There are ghosts lurking in the swamp, and fog witches live there, and if you don't hide in time . . ."

Then he remembered the elf.

"I've got to go!" he shouted, and ran off.

53

Small Fur ran to the bushes where the moving van had disappeared. He ran through the green gate. He ran through the honeyflower meadow. He ran all the way to the black pool. The Nock and the elf were sitting on the bank talking.

"What took you so long, Small Fur?" asked the Nock. "We have been waiting for you."

"I was playing with Curly Fur," said Small Fur, gasping for breath. "He lives in Brown Fur's house. He's smaller than me and he has a yellow ball."

"If you want to fly, you'll have to hurry," said the elf. "The day is almost over."

"Don't do it, Small Fur," gurgled the Nock. "Stay where you belong."

But Small Fur *wanted* to fly. He took the wings, and the wind carried him up into the air. He flew over forests and meadows and rivers. It was wonderful! He felt so good that nothing mattered anymore. He flew and flew until the sun set and the wind brought him back down.

56

57

"You stayed up there a long time," said the elf.

"It was so beautiful," said Small Fur.

"Come again tomorrow," she said. "And don't tell anyone about our gate, or it will disappear forever."

Small Fur went home past the birch trees and across the honeyflower meadow. Only then did he remember that he had forgotten to look for Brown Fur.

Tomorrow, he thought. There is still time tomorrow.

His mother came out to meet him. She wanted to know where he had been.

"In the forest," said Small Fur.

"And what have you been doing all this time?" she asked.

"Oh, nothing," he said.

There was raspberry pudding for supper, and Aunt Grouch was not home. Small Fur sat at the table with his mother. She hugged him, and Small Fur wished he could tell her all about the green gate and the elf and the Nock, and about flying. It's a shame I can't tell anyone about it, he thought.

The next day, when Small Fur went to meet
the elf, he forgot to take his red ball with him.
He didn't even notice he had left it behind.

Curly Fur stood in front of Brown Fur's house,
waving to him.

"I don't have time to play," said Small Fur.
"Well, maybe we could play a little."

They climbed up into the treehouse that Small Fur and Brown Fur had built. They chased a squirrel and threw pinecones down rabbit holes. Small Fur showed Curly Fur his favorite bee tree. He also showed him where tree ghosts sleep during the day and where the trolls live.

And so the morning passed.

"Let's play after lunch," said Curly Fur.

"I've got to be somewhere else," said Small Fur.

"Where?"

Small Fur didn't answer.

"Come on, tell me," begged Curly Fur.

"It's a secret," said Small Fur.

I wish I could tell him, he thought.

The elf was waiting for him. She gave him her wings and the wind took him away. Small Fur soared higher and higher, farther and farther into the light. He flew and forgot everything, even Brown Fur, and that he wanted to find him.

The elf and the Nock were sitting by the black pool when the wind brought him back.

"Do you want to fly again tomorrow?" asked the elf.

"Yes!" said Small Fur. "Every day."

"Every day? From morning until night? And forget everything?"

Small Fur nodded.

"Nonsense," gurgled the Nock.

The elf said, "My sisters will be here tomorrow. We will give you your own wings. Then you can fly anytime you want, and you will become transparent like us."

"Transparent?" Small Fur had to laugh. "Brown Fur will be surprised. So will Curly Fur."

"Don't do it," gurgled the Nock.

"Anyone who wants to fly *should* fly," said the elf.

They sat in the sun. The black water glinted, and the wind scattered the scent of the honeyflowers. Small Fur sniffed.

"What do elves eat?" he asked.

"Nothing," said the elf. "Elves don't eat."

"And where are your beds?"

"Nowhere," said the elf. "Elves don't need beds."

"Oh," said Small Fur. He liked to eat. He also liked to snuggle in his bed. He couldn't imagine someone not wanting either.

"And my mother? Will my mother recognize me when I'm transparent?"

"When you're transparent, you won't need a mother," said the elf. "No mother, no grouchy old aunt, no Brown Fur, no Curly Fur. All you'll ever want to do is fly. Fly and fly and fly."

"Oh," said Small Fur again. He didn't quite understand what she meant.

The Nock slid back into the water. He waved to Small Fur one more time with his green, weedy hand.

"Stay where you belong, Small Fur," he said.

"Everybody should be where he wants to be," said the elf.

That night, Mother and Aunt Grouch went into the forest to gather night herbs, which are good for coughs, stomachaches and bad

dreams.

Small Fur lay in his bed and thought. He thought about the green gate. He thought about the Nock down in the black pool. He thought about the elf who slept anywhere. The transparent elf.

Soon I'll be transparent, too, thought Small Fur. I wonder if it's comfortable sleeping on a gray rock. Probably very hard. And cold. But flying is wonderful. The most wonderful thing in the world.

After a while, Small Fur got out of bed. He pulled on his pants and went to Brown Fur's house, which was now Curly Fur's.

"Curly Fur," he called, "are you asleep?"

Curly Fur poked his head out the window.

"Not yet. I'll be right down."

They sat on the forest floor and counted the stars.

"So many stars," said Curly Fur, "there are just too many to count."

Small Fur was silent.

"Are you counting them with me?"

Small Fur didn't answer.

"Are you thinking about something?" asked Curly Fur.

Small Fur nodded.

"About something nice?"

"About my secret," said Small Fur.

Curly Fur shifted closer to him.

"But you're my friend," he said.

"You're my friend, too," said Small Fur. "Just as Brown Fur used to be. I don't have to look for him anymore because now I have you. But if I told you about the green gate, I'd never find it again, and then I would never be able to fly again. And flying is so wonderful."

Small Fur clapped his hand over his mouth. "I've told you my secret," he whispered.

He jumped up. He ran quickly through the dark forest to the spot where the moving van had disappeared and where he had last seen Brown Fur.

The moon was shining down on the trees and bushes. But the gate was gone! The green gate, the honeyflower meadow, the birch trees.

68   "Elf!" called Small Fur. "Elf!"

Nobody answered. Everything was still.
"Elf!" Small Fur called again.
The elf did not answer.

Small Fur sat down in the grass and cried.
"Don't be sad," Curly Fur said. He shifted closer to his friend.

But Small Fur kept on crying. He ran home. He lay in his bed, still crying.

"Everything will be all right," said his mother. She hugged him. She hugged him for a long, long time. And finally Small Fur fell asleep.

Time passed. Autumn came, then winter, and then summer again. Small Fur was no longer sad. He ate and drank and slept. He played with Curly Fur. Sometimes he was happy and sometimes he got mad. He was growing up.

But he never forgot the green gate, the honeyflower meadow, the Nock in his black pool, or the elf.

71

Sometimes he still dreams about flying. He flies over forests and meadows and rivers, higher and higher he soars into the light, and it is wonderful.